WRITTEN BY
AMY HEST

PICTURES BY
ELIVIA SAVADIER

BROADWAY

WHEN YOU MEET A BEAR
ON BROADWAY

Melanie Kroupa Books   Farrar, Straus and Giroux   New York

Love to Gloria

—A.H.

*For all my friends
at the Longfellow School*

—E.S.

When you meet a bear on Broadway, *this* is what to do.
Suck in your breath. Stick out your hand.
And say, "Stop there, Little Bear!"
And he will. Stop. Immediately. (To your great relief.)

"What is your business on Broadway?"
you ask. (You must ask this politely.)

"It's my mama. My mama is lost!"
He shivers and droops and
covers his eyes and cries. *"Boohoo!"*

Softly at first.
Then louder.

"BOOHOO!"

And louder still.

"BOOHOO!"

"You are making a racket," you say.
(But not unkindly.)
"Hush-a-bit, Little Bear.
So we can think."

And he does.
Hush-a-bit. And sniffle a bit.
He takes your hand.

Now find a bench and sit on the bench to think.
The two of you together.
The bench is cold and here you sit, swinging your legs.
Little Bear slides closer and you slide, too.

When you meet a bear on Broadway
and his mama is lost, *this* is what to ask.
"How does your mama look, Little Bear?"
"Oh!" he says. "Looks like Mama!"

And *this* is what to ask.
"How does your mama sing, Little Bear?"
"Oh!" he says. "Sings like Mama!"

But when you ask, "How does your mama hug, Little Bear?"
he springs off the bench.
And stamps his foot.
"Must hug Mama! Now!

NOW!
NOW!"

So off you go. The two of you.
To look for Little Bear's mama to hug.

You look uptown . . .

downtown . . .

and along the banks of the river . . .

until you find a park.
A fine, good park with grass and trees.
And a fine, tall tree for your bear to climb.

And up he climbs.
Up. And up. To the highest branch.
"Ma-maaa!" he sings.

AAAAAAAAAAAAAAAAAAAAAA!"

And his song sails off on the wings of the wind.
Across the park . . . along the banks of the river . . .
downtown . . . uptown . . . all the way to Broadway.
"Ma-maaa!"

"Little Bear!"
Her song comes softly at first.

Then louder.

"LITTLE BEAR!"

And louder still.

"LITTLE BEAR!!!"

The ground shakes. The trees shake.

And here she is. Little Bear's mama. Lost no more.
"Is it you, Little Bear? Is it really, really you?"

JUMP!
JUMP!

Little Bear jumps.

Into the arms of his mama.
Safe and warm.
"Oh!" he says. "Hugs like *Mama*!"

When you meet a bear on Broadway
and his mama is lost,
just take his hand
and surely you will find her.

Then say goodbye. (Politely.)
And wave. Until they are dots.

Now run! RUN! RUN!
On the wings of the wind. All the way home.

To tell your mama everything
that happened on this crispy-cold day.

Distributed in Canada by Douglas & McIntyre Ltd.
Color separations by Embassy Graphics
Printed in February 2009 in the United States of America
by Phoenix Color Corp. d/b/a Lehigh Phoenix–Rockaway, Rockaway, New Jersey
Designed by Irene Metaxatos
First edition, 2009
1   3   5   7   9   10   8   6   4   2

www.fsgkidsbooks.com

Library of Congress Cataloging-in-Publication Data
Hest, Amy.
    When you meet a bear on Broadway / Amy Hest ; pictures by Elivia Savadier.— 1st ed.
        p.   cm.
    Summary: When a little bear becomes separated from its mother in New York, a
sympathetic child explains the proper steps that must be taken to reunite them.
    ISBN-13: 978-0-374-40015-6
    ISBN-10: 0-374-40015-6
    [1. Bears—Fiction.   2. Lost children—Fiction.   3. Mother and child—Fiction.
4. New York (N.Y.)—Fiction.]   I. Savadier, Elivia, ill.   II. Title.

PZ7.H4375 Wg 2009
[E]—dc22
                                                                    2008026053

Paint